OCT - - 2013

SAMMY
the
Dragon

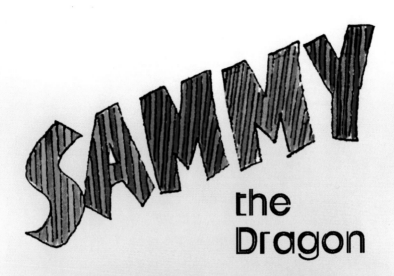

In loving memory of Jimmy,
the inspiration for this book.

Grateful Steps, Inc.
159 South Lexington Avenue
Asheville, North Carolina 28801

Copyright © 2011 by Anne Marone
Library of Congress Control Number: 2011931105

Marone, Anne
Sammy the Dragon

Drawings Illustrator, John ("Jack") Ferrell – sketches
Graphic Designer, Syvanah Bennett – color/design
Layout and design by Sundara Fawn

ISBN 978-1-935130-42-0
Printed in the United States of America
United Graphics, Inc., Mattoon Illinois

FIRST EDITION

www.gratefulsteps.com

SAMMY
the
Dragon

by Anne Marone

Grateful Steps, Inc.
Asheville, North Carolina

Sammy the Dragon
Spent his time alone
In a dark and gloomy cave
He lovingly called home.

Sammy was green and scaly,
And when his nostrils opened wide,
Fire and smoke came flying out
From somewhere deep inside.

Most of the forest animals
Would run and play all day
As Sammy quietly watched them
And hoped someday they'd say,

"We know you are different,
But you can come and play.
The sun is bright, the weather just right,
Come join us this fine day."

Sammy didn't have a friend,
And all would shake with fear.
They would hide behind the rocks and trees
When Sammy would come near.

So Sammy patiently waited,
But there never came a day
When any of the animals
Would let poor Sammy play.

Summer was soon over.
The leaves fell from the trees,
And a cold and chilly wind
Replaced the summer breeze.

Then it started snowing.
It didn't stop all day,
And all the little animals
Couldn't come out to play.

The animals got hungry
They hardly could keep warm.
They couldn't look for food
In the cold and wintry storm.

Sammy came out to look for them.
His nostrils opened wide,
And lots of fire and smoke
Came from somewhere deep inside.

He melted snow and warmed the air
With his mighty flame,
And one by one because of the warmth
The little animals came.

Sammy snorted once again
And melted some more snow,
And all the little animals
Were warmed by the fiery glow.

They found some nuts, some twigs and treats.
It was a happy day,
And Sammy was the happiest
Because they let him play.

He motioned for them to climb on his back,
To slide and play in the snow.
And when they were cold, he proudly snorted
And let his nostrils blow.

The animals came to understand,
That Sammy was their friend.
He was there to help them.
On him, they could depend.

Sometimes children are different
In color or in size—
Sometimes their noses, their mouths or teeth,
Or maybe the shape of their eyes.

But you can share a friendly smile
And ask them to come and play.
You'll find you have some nice new friends

. . .To help you enjoy the day!

Topics for discussion

1. The story about Sammy is a fiction story. Do you know what the word "fiction" means?

2. Let's talk about some of the things in the story that helped you to decide whether or not the book is a fiction book.

3. Can you name some of the things that Sammy could do that the animals could not do?

4. Without looking back, can you name the animals in the story?

5. How was Sammy different from the other animals in the story?

6. In the beginning of the story Sammy was not very happy. Why was Sammy sad?

7. The animals felt differently about Sammy at the end of the story. Do you know why?

8. Would you be a friend to another child who was different from you in some way? Why or why not?

9. Rhyming words all have the same endings. Can you find rhyming words in the story?

Be on the lookout for Sammy's next adventure!

Anne Marone-Ianni is a retired
teacher who created Sammy
and his animal friends to help
her young students learn about
and appreciate the differences in
others. She is the mother of four,
grandmother of six, and resides
with her husband in New Jersey.
Anne plans to publish additional
books about Sammy, exploring
issues young children face as they
grow and learn.